NO!

David McPhail

FRANCES LINCOLN
CHILDREN'S BOOKS

For teachers everywhere.

Text and illustrations copyright © David McPhail 2009
The right of David McPhail to be identified as the author and illustrator of this work
has been asserted by him in accordance with the Copyright, Designs and Patents Act, 1988 (United Kingdom).

First published in the USA by Roaring Brook Press
Roaring Book Press is a division of Holtzbrinck Publishing Holdings Limited Partnership
175 Fifth Avenue, New York, New York 10010
All rights reserved

First published in Great Britain in 2011 by
Frances Lincoln Children's Books, 4 Torriano Mews,
Torriano Avenue, London NW5 2RZ
www.franceslincoln.com

A catalogue record for this book is available from the British Library.

ISBN 978-1-84780-120-3

Printed in China

1 3 5 7 9 8 6 4 2

Everyone has the right to be safe and to be treated fairly. But sometimes people can be cruel. And we need to say "No!" when we see things that are wrong, just like the boy in this book.

Amnesty International wants everybody in the world to enjoy all their rights. If people are being hurt and if their rights are being taken away, it is Amnesty who says "No" and works to make things better. We try to tell the world how important rights are.

Lots of our supporters are children.

You can find out more at www.amnesty.org.uk/education

Amnesty International UK
The Human Rights Action Centre
17–25 New Inn Yard
London EC2A 3EA
Tel: 020 7033 1500